MILLIONS OF CATS

BY WANDA GÁG

PUFFIN BOOKS

PUFFIN BOOKS
Published by the Penguin Group
Penguin Young Readers Group, 345 Hudson Street, New York, New York 10014, U.S.A.
Penguin Group (Canada), 90 Eglinton Avenue East, Suite 700, Toronto, Ontario, Canada M4P 2Y3
(a division of Pearson Penguin Canada Inc.)
Penguin Books Ltd, 80 Strand, London WC2R 0RL, England
Penguin Ireland, 25 St Stephen's Green, Dublin 2, Ireland
(a division of Penguin Books Ltd)
Penguin Group (Australia), 250 Camberwell Road, Camberwell, Victoria 3124, Australia
(a division of Pearson Australia Group Pty Ltd)
Penguin Books India Pvt Ltd, 11 Community Centre, Panchsheel Park, New Delhi - 110 017, India
Penguin Group (NZ), Cnr Airborne and Rosedale Roads, Albany, Auckland 1310, New Zealand
(a division of Pearson New Zealand Ltd)
Penguin Books (South Africa) (Pty) Ltd, 24 Sturdee Avenue, Rosebank, Johannesburg 2196, South Africa

Registered Offices: Penguin Books Ltd, 80 Strand, London WC2R 0RL, England

First published in the United States of America by Coward-McCann, Inc., New York, in 1928.
Published by Puffin Books, a division of Penguin Young Readers Group, 2006

7 9 10 8 6

Puffin Books ISBN 0-14-240708-9
Manufactured in China

MILLIONS OF CATS

Once upon a time there was a very old man and a very old woman. They lived in a nice clean house which had flowers

all around it, except where the door was. But they couldn't be happy because they were so very lonely.

"If we only had a cat!" sighed the very old woman.

"A cat?" asked the very old man.

"Yes, a sweet little fluffy cat," said the very old woman.

"I will get you a cat, my dear," said the very old man.

And he set out over the hills to look for one. He climbed over the sunny hills. He trudged through the cool valleys. He walked a long, long time and at last he came to a hill which was quite covered with cats.

Cats here, cats there,
Cats and kittens everywhere,
Hundreds of cats,
Thousands of cats,
Millions and billions and trillions of cats.

"Oh," cried the old man joyfully, "Now I can choose the prettiest cat and take it home with me!" So he chose one. It was white. But just as he was about to leave, he saw another one all black and white and it seemed just as pretty as the first. So he took this one also.

But then he saw a fuzzy grey kitten way over here which was every bit as pretty as the others so he took it too.

And now he saw one way down in a cor- ner which he thought too lovely to leave so he took this too.

And just then, over here, the very old man found a kitten which was black and very beautiful.

"It would be a shame to leave that one," said the very old man. So he took it.

And now, over there,
he saw a cat which had
brown and yellow stripes
like a baby tiger.
"I simply must take
it!" cried the very old
man, and he did.

So it happened that every
time the very old man looked
up, he saw another cat which
was so pretty he could not
bear to leave it, and before he
knew it, he had chosen them all

And so he went back over the sunny hills and down through the cool valleys, to show all his pretty kittens to the very old woman.

It was very funny to see those hundreds and thousands and millions and billions and trillions of cats following him.

They came to a pond.
"Mew, mew! We are thirsty!" cried the
Hundreds of cats,
Thousands of cats,
Millions and billions and trillions of cats.

"Well, here is a great deal of water,"
said the very old man.
　　Each cat took a sip of water, and
the pond was gone!

"Mew, mew! Now we are hungry!" said the
Hundreds of cats,
Thousands of cats,
Millions and billions and trillions of cats.

"There is much grass on the hills," said the very old man.

Each cat ate a mouthful of grass and not a blade was left!

Pretty soon the very old woman saw them coming.

"My dear!" she cried, "What are you doing? I asked for one little cat, and what do I see? —

" Cats here, cats there,
Cats and kittens everywhere,
Hundreds of cats,
Thousands of cats,
Millions and billions and trillions of cats.

"But we can never feed them all," said the very old woman, "They will eat us out of house and home."

"I never thought of that," said the very old man, "What shall we do?"

The very old woman thought for a while and then she said, "I know! We will let the cats decide which one we should keep."

"Oh yes," said the very old man, and he called to the cats, "Which one of you is the prettiest?"

"I am!"

"I am!"

"No, I am!"

"No, I am the prettiest!" "I am!"

"No, I am! I am! I am!" cried hundreds and thousands and millions and billions and trillions of voices, for each cat thought itself the prettiest.

And they began to quarrel.

They bit and scratched and clawed each other and made such a great noise that the very old man and the very old woman ran into the house as fast as they could. They did not like such quarreling. But after a while the noise stopped and the very old man and the very old woman peeped out of the window to see what had happened. They could not see a single cat!

"I think
they must
have eaten
each other all up,"
said the very old
woman, "It's too bad!"
"But look!" said the
very old man, and he
pointed to a bunch of
high grass. In it sat one
little frightened kitten.
They went out and picked
it up. It was thin and scraggly.

"Poor little kitty," said the very old woman
"Dear little kitty," said the very old man, "how does it happen that you were not eaten up with all those hundreds and thousands and millions and billions and trillions of cats?"
"Oh, I'm just a very homely little cat," said the kitten," So when you asked who was the prettiest, I didn't say anything. So nobody bothered about me."

They took the kitten into the house, where the very old woman gave it a warm bath and brushed its fur until it was soft and shiny.

Every day they gave
it plenty of
milk—

—and soon it grew
nice and
plump.

"And it is a very pretty cat, after all!" said the very old woman.
"It is the most beautiful cat in the whole world," said the very old man. "I ought to know, for I've seen—
Hundreds of cats,
Thousands of cats,
Millions and billions and trillions of cats—
and not one was as pretty as this one."